D1442486

Sweet Child o' Mine

Sweet Child o' Mine

the ADVENTURES OF Maya and NatAlia Rose

GUNS N' ROSES

ILLUSTRATED BY JENNIFER ZIVOIN

jimmy patterson

JIMMY Patterson Books
Little, Brown and Company
New York Boston London

She's got a smile that it seems to me
reminds me of childhood memories,

where everything

was as fresh as the bright blue sky.

Now and then when I see her face,
she takes me away to that special place,

and if I stared too long,
I'd probably break down and cry.

Oh, sweet child o' mine.

Oh, sweet love of mine.

She's got eyes of the bluest skies,
as if they thought of rain.

I'd hate to look into those eyes
and see an ounce of pain.

Her hair reminds me of
a warm, safe place
where as a child I'd hide

and pray for the thunder
and the rain
to quietly pass me by.

Oh, sweet child o' mine.
Oh, sweet love of mine.

Where do we go?

Where do we go now?

Where do we go?

Sweet child.

Sweet child o' mine.

Copyright © 2020 by Lebeis Publishing, Inc.

Hachette Book Group supports the right to free expression and the value of copyright. The purpose of copyright is to encourage writers and artists to produce the creative works that enrich our culture.The scanning, uploading, and distribution of this book without permission is a theft of the authors' intellectual property. If you would like permission to use material from the book (other than for review purposes), please contact permissions@hbgusa.com. Thank you for your support of the authors' rights.

JIMMY Patterson Books / Little, Brown and Company / Hachette Book Group / 1290 Avenue of the Americas, New York, NY 10104 / JamesPatterson.com

First Edition: September 2020

JIMMY Patterson Books is an imprint of Little, Brown and Company, a division of Hachette Book Group, Inc. The Little, Brown name and logo are trademarks of Hachette Book Group, Inc. The JIMMY Patterson Books® name and logo are trademarks of JBP Business, LLC.

The publisher is not responsible for websites (or their content) that are not owned by the publisher.
The Hachette Speakers Bureau provides a wide range of authors for speaking events. To find out more, go to hachettespeakersbureau.com or call (866) 376-6591.

Library of Congress Cataloging-in-Publication Data
Names: Guns N' Roses (Musical group), author. | Zivoin, Jennifer, illustrator | Title: Sweet child o' mine / Guns N' Roses ; illustrated by Jennifer Zivoin.
Other titles: Sweet child of mine | Description: First edition. | New York : Jimmy Patterson Books/Little, Brown and Company, 2020. | Audience: Ages 2-6.
| Audience: Grades K–1. | Summary: Celebrates the love between a parent and child through an illustrated retelling of song lyrics from Guns N' Roses.
Identifiers: LCCN 2019044346 (print) | LCCN 2019044347 (ebook) | ISBN 9780316493352 (hardcover) | ISBN 9780316493338 (ebook)
Subjects: LCSH: Children's songs—Texts. | CYAC: Parent and child—Songs and music. | Songs.
Classification: LCC PZ8.3.G9575 Swe 2020 (print) | LCC PZ8.3.G9575 (ebook) | DDC 782.42—dc23
LC record available at https://lccn.loc.gov/2019044346
LC ebook record available at https://lccn.loc.gov/2019044347

10 9 8 7 6 5 4 3 2 1

Printed in China